To Katmandu
A STORY OF NEPAL

THOMAS Y. CROWELL COMPANY
NEW YORK

To Katmandu

A STORY OF NEPAL

By ARNOLD DOBRIN
illustrated by the author

STORIES FROM MANY LANDS

THE GOATS WHO KILLED THE LEOPARD: *A Story of Ethiopia*
by Judy Hawes

THE GREEN, GREEN SEA: *A Story of Greece*
by Molly Cone

MIKA'S APPLE TREE: *A Story of Finland*
by Clyde Robert Bulla

THE MOST TERRIBLE TURK: *A Story of Turkey*
by Joseph Krumgold

NEW BOY IN DUBLIN: *A Story of Ireland*
by Clyde Robert Bulla

THE TWO HATS: *A Story of Portugal*
by Roland Bertol

MAKOTO, THE SMALLEST BOY: *A Story of Japan*
by Yoshiko Uchida

TO KATMANDU: *A Story of Nepal*
by Arnold Dobrin

THE HOUSE IN THE TREE: *A Story of Israel*
by Molly Cone

MANUFACTURED IN THE UNITED STATES OF AMERICA

L.C. Card 74-132296
ISBN 0-690-82730-X
0-690-82731-8 (LB)

1 2 3 4 5 6 7 8 9 10

To Katmandu
A STORY OF NEPAL

"Come, Sanu—*come!*"

Turning to the sound of his brother's voice, Sanu ran to the door and opened it. He looked down to the bottom of the steps where Ram was standing with a serious look in his brown eyes. He was a happy boy, usually grinning and laughing. But now he was not laughing.

"What is the matter?" Sanu asked.

"Come and see."

Sanu went down the steps two at a time and into the first floor of their house where the animals lived. Ram followed him inside. The bullocks were already at work in the fields with Father. Their stalls were empty.

Sanu smelled the familiar odor of straw and dust and bullock dung. He ran through the warm April sunlight that buzzed with dozens of flies. But even before he got to the far corner of the stall, Sanu knew why Ram had such a serious look on his face.

Sanu knelt down. In one corner of the straw was his brown puppy, curled up and lying very still. As he started to reach out for it Ram said, "He is dead."

Sanu did not cry. The puppy had been sick ever since Ram first brought him home. For the last two days he lay weakly in the straw, and from time to time he whimpered. Sanu had tried to give him some warm buffalo milk, but he refused to drink it.

Sanu turned to his brother. "Ram," he asked sadly, "Why did he die?"

Ram was squatting near the dead puppy. "He was sick. He died."

"But *why?*"

"He was sick. He died," Ram repeated as he picked up the puppy. "Things just happen. You ask too many questions." He started to carry the small dog out to the fields.

Sanu knew that he asked too many questions. Everybody was telling him so all the time. There were always so many things he wanted to know. But one thing he did not want to know was where Ram was taking the puppy or what he was going to do with him.

While Ram was gone, Sanu sat in the doorway watching some blue wisps of smoke curling up in the sky from the road beyond the house. He tried not to think about his puppy. He thought about his work in the fields. Sanu knew that he should get his hoe and start weeding. He had just forced himself to stand up when Ram appeared.

"Does Father know?" Sanu asked.

"Yes," Ram replied. "He saw before he went into the fields. And he said you could come with me today if you want to. But you will have to help me carry some of the vegetables."

"To Katmandu?" Sanu asked eagerly.

"Yes." Ram's eyes twinkled for the first time this morning as he grinned and said, "Why not? In a few years you will be old enough to go to Katmandu by yourself. Anyway, I can use some help with the vegetables."

At the edge of the field were piles of cucumbers and radishes that the boys' father had just finished stacking. Earlier, Mother had taken another load to the city to sell. Now Ram filled two big baskets for himself and two small ones for Sanu. He tied the small baskets to a pole and helped Sanu to place it across his shoulders. Then he did the same for himself.

Together they walked through the fields in the gentle spring sunshine. The morning breeze was sweet with the fragrance of millions of new blossoms. Insects buzzed loudly in the warm, clear air.

As they came nearer the road Sanu smelled food cooking. He remembered the blue wisps of smoke that he had seen coming from the road earlier in the morning, and he knew that either a caravan or some pilgrims were camped by the roadside.

As soon as they turned out of the lane Sanu saw about a dozen Indian women who had stopped to have their breakfast. They wore brightly colored saris and had gold rings in their nostrils. Some of them wore heavy gold anklets and earrings too.

"*Namaste*," good morning, Sanu said, putting the palms of his hands together near his chest. Ram also said, "*Namaste*," as he did the same thing with his hands. The women returned the greeting.

Sanu smelled the delicious odor of spices that drifted through the fresh morning air. He saw the steaming mounds of food being eaten from the broad green leaves that were used as plates. And for the first time this morning he felt hungry. But now he would have to wait until they reached Katmandu. Already Ram was starting out along the road to the capital. Sanu hurried to catch up.

As they walked, Sanu remembered what his grandmother had told him about the pilgrims

who were often on the roads. Unlike Ram—who was sometimes very impatient with Sanu—Sanu's grandmother always answered his questions carefully.

It wasn't the first time she had explained, "Men who are holy leave a little of themselves in the holy places they visit. Then these places become even *more* holy. And when ordinary people like you or me, or your mother or father, or Ram, visit these places we become holier too."

"Just by going there?" Sanu asked.

"Yes," his grandmother answered, "just by going. But it is better to go with a pure heart—and to pray for greater purity and love."

Then a great many people were looking for purity and love, Sanu thought, because the road just beyond his father's farm was always full of pilgrims. Some came from as far away as Ceylon, his grandmother said. She, too, often talked of making a long pilgrimage, but until now she had never left the valley of Katmandu.

"Ceylon, Ceylon," Sanu repeated to himself.

What a strange kind of name! But just as he was saying "Ceylon, Ceylon," he looked up and saw some distant towers in the morning haze. They were the pagodas of Katmandu.

Sanu could smell the bazaar even before he came to the bustling, noisy square. People were looking, or buying or selling, or just strolling around and chatting. The shops flashed with color—the colors of bright printed cloths, of gleaming brass pots, of huge mounds of shining fruit and vegetables.

Almost in the middle of the bazaar a sacred white cow munched some tender grasses that grew from cracks in the pavement. Sanu sniffed the delicious spicy smells of saffron and ginger and felt even hungrier.

Sanu thought his mother would be surprised to see him, but if she was, she did not show it. He unloaded his basket of vegetables very carefully and then, without thinking what he was going to say, blurted out, "My puppy died."

"Yes, I know."

"I'm hungry," Sanu said.

"One *chatamari* for each," his mother said as she gave them a rupee. "Then home to work."

"Yes, Mother." And while she turned to help a customer who had just appeared, Sanu and Ram walked quickly to the foodseller's stand. The *chatamaries*—whole-wheat pancakes—were rolled over delicious hot chili pickles. They disappeared much too fast. But Ram was all grins. "Come on, Sanu," he said, "We've got work to do at home. But I think that first we will take a look around Katmandu—all right?"

It was very all right with Sanu. He loved
the bustle and confusion of the city, loved its
many temples and palaces and all the foods
and odors of the streets. Although he had
visited Katmandu before, he could be sure to
see new things whenever he came. Especially
at the bazaar.

"See that?" Ram said, pointing to a small,
boxlike object with metal coils on the top.
"Do you know what it is?"

Sanu thought. "A radio?" he asked.

Ram laughed. "Of course not."

Sanu thought again. "It's . . . it's just a box."

"No, no," Ram said, "It's a *stove.*"

That seemed impossible. "How can a little box like that be a stove?" he demanded of Ram.

"Do you see that thing like a long black snake coiled next to it?"

Sanu hadn't seen it, but now he did.

"It is for electricity," Ram explained, proud that he knew such things. Oh well, thought Sanu, Ram was always talking about strange matters. Sanu loved to hear about them but sometimes he pretended not to care. Now he started to move away down an unfamiliar street. Ram followed. Soon they were in a section of the city Sanu had never seen before.

They turned a corner. Beyond was a small square full of men. Sanu and Ram stopped to look and listen.

At first Sanu thought that all the men standing so quietly in the square were Nepali, like himself. Soon he saw that many of the men were Sherpas, the people who live high in the mountains of Nepal.

Sanu slipped through the crowd of men to the far side of the square, where he heard loud voices. Near a wall, at three small tables, sat two big yellow-haired men and one big red-haired man from another country. One man had a very pink skin, but all of them reminded Sanu of raw potatoes before they are put into the oven and nicely browned. He was not sure he liked these strange, uncooked faces so different from the warm, golden-brown skins of the Nepali.

Ram whispered, "They are mountain climbers."

"But what are they doing here?" asked Sanu.

"What do you think?" Ram demanded impatiently. "They are hiring the Sherpas to work as porters." Then Sanu remembered that the Sherpas were the best porters in all of Nepal. He listened to the man with the red beard speak first in Nepali and then in a language he did not understand. He was just going to ask Ram what it was when Ram said, "English!"

Sanu and Ram stood for a long time watching. They wished they could go up and touch the strange-looking clothing being shown to the porters. Sanu was amazed at the crates full of thick, curious ropes, boots, and dozens of other things he had never seen before. How he would love to wear the bright blue or yellow jackets and join the men on their journey in the high mountains. Sanu wanted to stay all day, but soon Ram was tugging at his arm. It was time to return to the farm and to work.

The noon sun was strong. Sanu and Ram walked slowly, thinking of all the sights they had seen. It was hard to think of work on such a spring morning. The air was so clear that the mountains to the north of the road seemed closer than ever. Even through the hottest summers their high peaks remained covered with glistening white snow.

It was strange. Sanu was hot, he was sweating. Yet the snow on the mountains remained

frozen. Ram would know about that. He was seventeen and he knew so many things— although Sanu was still not sure he was right about the stove.

"Ram," he asked as they walked along the dusty road, "Why are the tops of the mountains *always* white with snow?"

Ram decided that he must try to be patient. In a gentle voice he answered, "The mountains are very high. It is always cold so high." Then he added proudly, "The Himalayas are the highest mountains in the world. The one the Sherpas call the Goddess of the Wind is the highest mountain of all."

Sanu asked excitedly, "And these mountains are in *our* country?"

"Not exactly," Ram answered. "Part of the Himalayas are in Nepal, yes—but a part of them are in Tibet."

That was very confusing. Where did countries end and where did they begin? The maps Sanu saw in school had pretty colors on them, and interesting shapes, but they were still *very* confusing. Only two things were clear in his mind about the world beyond Nepal—Tibet was to the north, India was to the south. And the Tibetans and Indians were always crossing Nepal to get from one place to the other!

Yes, the road was a busy place. Although the pilgrims from India who had been camped near the roadside in the morning were gone, some other people had taken their place. Seeing their fur-trimmed hats, Sanu knew at once that they were Tibetans.

Their yaks and mules were heavily loaded with things which the Tibetans hoped to sell in India. Sanu could hear the faint, sweet tinkling of the bells as the animals searched along the roadside for grass to eat.

"Namaste," Sanu greeted the Tibetans.

"Namaste." The wrinkled faces of the traders showed that they were no longer young, but their eyes twinkled and their teeth were white and strong.

"What is in the pouches?" Sanu asked.

"There is wool. Some furs."

"And when you return to Tibet, what will you put in the pouches?" Sanu asked.

The eyes of the Tibetan traders twinkled again. "Very precious things. Turquoise. Rhinoceros horns."

"But who would buy those?" Sanu asked.

"Chinese herb doctors pay much for them," one of the men explained. "They make good medicine." But Sanu had stopped listening

because he heard the whimpering sounds of a small animal coming from the pouches.

The Tibetan's eyes followed Sanu's gaze. "You want to see?" he asked.

"Yes."

The trader unstrapped a pouch and lifted the leather flap. There were two of the most beautiful, plump mastiff puppies Sanu had ever seen.

Carefully, gently, he patted their thick,

glossy fur. Sanu thought of the puppy that had died. Its poor thin body had never felt like this. Sanu continued petting the mastiff. He was just going to ask if he could hold it when the Tibetan came over to close the pouch. Soon the caravan would be leaving.

That night Sanu could not sleep. For a long time he lay in bed thinking about the strange sights and men he had seen during the day. He kept seeing the faces of the foreign mountain climbers, the color of raw potatoes. He saw the Sherpas standing quietly near the walls, hoping to be chosen for the expedition. He remembered the big crates of equipment that were being packed with shiny hooks and thick ropes, bright-colored clothing, and the heaviest boots he had ever seen.

Sanu wondered if they were going to climb the Goddess of the Wind. He could see the dazzling white snow, feel the cold winds around his face . . . yes, *his* face, for he too was a part of the expedition. He would struggle with the men as they pressed ahead toward the summit of the mountain. Why not? Sanu could help. He could be a mountain climber if he wanted to. And maybe he would be soon!

There were many things he could do. He might even join the pilgrims from the great world beyond Nepal. Perhaps he would go down into India or Ceylon.

Or Japan.

Or maybe he would join one of the caravans and go into Tibet. The world was very big and wonderful. Sanu wanted to see all of it. And of course he would. He knew he could do anything if he really wanted to.

As Sanu drifted into sleep, he thought of the mastiff puppies curled up in the basket. How sleek and beautiful they were! They would be fierce and very strong when they grew up, but if he had one, he would teach it to be gentle. He knew he could do that too.

The last thoughts Sanu had were about something that he had tried not to think about all through the day. Still, these thoughts were always in the back of his mind, just waiting, waiting to be remembered.

He saw his brown puppy now. First he saw it lying still and dead. Then he remembered how he had tried to play with it even though it was not frisky. He remembered how he had touched the puppy's hot, dry nose. He felt two warm tears slipping slowly down his cheeks. But then he felt nothing at all, because just as another tear began to form, Sanu fell asleep.

The next morning Sanu was up early. After tea and a light snack, which he ate with the rest of the family, he went to work in the fields weeding. His mother had gone to

Katmandu early with a load of vegetables. Ram would take her some more later in the day. The rest of the time he worked with Father in the fields so that another crop could soon be planted. Only Sanu's grandmother stayed in the house, to cook.

About ten o'clock they stopped for a big breakfast. There was a delicious vegetable curry mixed with rice, and big cups of cold

water. Occasionally a tiny bit of goat or buffalo meat was mixed into the curry, but Sanu was not sure that he liked eating meat. When he did, he thought of how beautiful and strong the animal had been when it was alive. Some priests—but not all—said it was sinful to kill animals for food.

After breakfast Sanu helped his grandmother tend to her pumpkin and cucumber vines, which grew on the thatched roof of their house. The warm sun felt good, but it was

much hotter than yesterday. Summer would come soon.

Sanu saw some blue wisps of smoke coming from the road again. Remembering the Tibetans he said, "A caravan passed by yesterday."

"Oh yes," his grandmother said, "Many caravans pass in the spring."

"The Tibetans had puppies to sell."

"Tibetan dogs bring a good price in Katmandu," Sanu's grandmother said as she snipped some vines.

"Why?"

"The dogs grow strong and ferocious. You have seen them, Sanu. No thief will try to steal from a house that is protected by a mastiff."

"I would like to have a puppy," Sanu said.

"Those dogs are for rich people." Sanu's grandmother slowly and carefully stepped down from a little stool she had been standing on and sighed. She seemed tired. Grey wisps of her hair fell around her face.

Sanu looked at her carefully. He said, "Grandmother, you are getting old. Why don't you go on a pilgrimage? You always talk of going to see the Bo tree where Buddha found enlightenment."

The old woman smiled. "Life passes quickly.

Sometimes there is not time enough for every-thing."

"Is it far to the Bo tree?" Sanu asked.

"Very far," his grandmother answered.

"Where?" Sanu asked.

"The tree itself died long ago. The one I would like to see grew from a sprig of the original tree. But even so, it is holy—very holy. It is on the island called Ceylon," Sanu's grandmother answered patiently.

"How long would it take to walk there?" Sanu asked.

How long? It was a question which Sanu's grandmother did not think about very much. "Months . . . years," she answered. "When you begin a pilgrimage to a holy place time does not matter."

"When will you go, Grandmother?"

Sanu's grandmother smiled again, "I must go soon or I shall not go at all. Perhaps I am too old already. But I shall try." She took a large brass urn and started down the road to the fountain. "Now," she said, "back to work, Sanu. Go."

Gradually the delicate leaves and flowers of spring changed. Their colors grew stronger, their petals larger. Summer had come, and with it, the great rains of the monsoon. They turned the rice fields near the house into watery lakes that reflected the sky and the dark, swiftly moving clouds. The weather was so hot and sticky that Sanu was glad when the crisp, cool days of autumn came.

During the Hindu festival of Tihar everyone decorated their houses and exploded fireworks. Some of the festivals were Hindu but

others were Buddhist. Sanu and his family were not exactly sure which was which. But that is the way it is in Nepal—both religions are mixed into one.

After Tihar, the days were colder. It never snowed where Sanu lived, but the mountains were whiter with every passing day. Sanu often looked toward the Himalayas now, thinking that no climber would dare to approach them at this time of the year. But in the spring surely they would come again.

An idea darted into Sanu's thoughts. Next year he would be nine. And strong. And big for his age. Why couldn't he join them? He would be a good mountain climber—he was certain of that.

Winter passed slowly. Twice Sanu went to Katmandu, but he did not see the square where the potato-faced men had sat so seriously with their crates full of equipment. Sanu waited, he waited impatiently. When the first warm days of spring appeared, he knew exactly what he was going to do.

The April morning was cool and silent. Without telling anyone that he was leaving, Sanu ran down the path to the road. His family would worry when they found that he was gone. But he would try to be home by noon —and then he would explain. When he did, and when he told them what had happened, they might even smile and say what a clever boy he was.

Sanu turned a bend in the road. Some thistles caught in his foot. He reached down as quickly as he could and plucked them out. Another time he would have sat down and rubbed his feet. There wasn't time for that now.

His feet flew on the hard, well-worn road. Sanu ran for a long time. He ran as fast as he could. He ran until he thought his heart might burst in his chest. And suddenly he felt stupid because he realized he could not possibly run all the way to Katmandu.

He slowed down and tried to take long but even steps. After a while his legs seemed to move by themselves while his mind was somewhere else. It seemed far off. It seemed to have already leaped ahead to Katmandu, where he was searching for the mountain climbers. There was one of the pagodas ahead in the morning mist! Sanu started to run again—but this time at a steady pace. As his legs pumped up and down, up and down, he looked neither to the left or right but continued steadily on his way to the capital.

Would the mountain climbers be there? Maybe they had come very early this year and were already climbing the steep, icy slopes of the Goddess of the Wind. Sanu hoped not. He, too, wanted to see her white vastness around him. He yearned to be one of the mountain climbers inching their way over her immense crags.

When Sanu came to the bazaar, people turned to look with amazement at the small boy running as though all the devils in Tibet were chasing him. Chickens in cages squawked and a sacred white cow excitedly lurched toward a building to avoid the small darting shape of the boy.

Sanu turned a corner that looked as though it led to the square where the climbers were, but instead he found himself in a maze of little alleyways. He returned to the central bazaar and tried again. This time he flew around the corner so swiftly that he almost overturned a basket of eggs. But now—*yes,* he had found it! He'd found the right street!

As he hurried down it toward the square his heart was pounding faster than it ever had before. Sanu could hardly catch his breath. But he was in luck. The mountain climbers were in Katmandu!

They were sitting at the same tables as before. Not the same men as last year, but men who had the same potato-colored faces and yellow hair. They were talking to the Sherpa porters and shuffling through papers.

Some of the men were trying on strange, frightening masks with big glass eyes which they could look through. Sanu wondered what they were. He wondered what devils' masks could have to do with mountain climbing. Some of the Sherpas were laughing as they tried on the shiny blue or yellow jackets.

Sanu watched. He waited, waited impatiently until his heart stopped beating so fast. But how long it was taking to quiet down!

While he was trying to catch his breath he remained on the outer edge of the group. None of the men noticed him. They did not notice him even as he walked closer to the tables. They did not notice him until he was almost standing so close to one of the little tables that he could touch it. Only then did one of the yellow-haired men look up from his papers.

"And what can I do for you, young man?" he asked in Nepali.

Sanu's heart started to beat fast all over again. It seemed not to be in his chest at all but in his mouth. Still, if he gulped hard enough, he found that he could speak. "Sir . . . I want to be a mountain climber. I want to climb the Goddess of the Wind. I am strong and I can be of help."

Now all the other men had stopped to listen and were looking at Sanu. The Sherpas were quiet too. Suddenly Sanu's voice sounded very loud, though it seemed to him that he was not talking much above a whisper.

The man pursed his lips and looked very serious. His light blue eyes darted quickly to the man sitting next to him. Then he said, "You are not a Sherpa boy, are you?"

"No, sir. I am a Nepali from Katmandu."

The man looked very serious. He said, "Sherpas make the best porters. They are used to living in high altitudes. They know how to work where the air is thin."

"But I can carry loads, sir. And I am strong. And . . . maybe, if I can't carry as much as a man, I can do other things like . . . like . . . well, I can make tea at the end of the day. I know how to make good tea."

"Yes," the man said seriously, "and what else can you do?"

"Oh." Sanu thought for a minute or two, wondering what to say. "I can sing. I know a lot of songs . . . and I can tell stories to make you laugh."

"Yes, and what else?"

Sanu thought for a moment. There was a loud silence in the square. "Nothing else, sir."

Suddenly the man's serious face broke into the widest, reddest grin Sanu had ever seen. "Oh, I am sure you could make me laugh," he said. "Oh . . . aahaaa . . ." The man seemed to be trying to keep from laughing now. He leaned back on the legs of his chair and clapped

the palms of his hands together. "You're a fine boy. But you are not old enough to be a mountain climber—yet."

The other potato-faced men had listened to their conversation. The Sherpas also began to understand what the talk was about. Sanu froze as he heard the laughter, for the men—all of them—were beginning to laugh. Laugh at *him*! The loud, horrible sound beat against his head. It hammered itself into his brain. The men were laughing and grinning and slapping each other's shoulders. Sanu seemed to hear—but from far, far away now—the potato-faced man saying, "You'll be a mountain climber, my boy, if you want to be one—but please wait a few years!"

Sanu did not want to hear any more. The only thing he wanted to do was run—run as fast as he could to get away from those terrible laughing faces and laughing voices.

He dashed out of the square, not knowing where he was going or what he was going to do. He only knew that he wanted to hide, to not be seen by anyone who could laugh at him. He skirted the central bazaar and walked through the back streets of Katmandu.

In this part of the city the streets were dirty. Sanu smelled a strange odor of rotted fruit or vegetables or—exactly what it was he didn't know. After a while the street became just an alley and then a dirt path leading out of the town. Now Sanu could see the fields and farms in the distance.

He came to the watery rice fields. When he waded through a ditch his feet were cooled by the water that had collected in it. He wished the rest of his body could feel as cool. But whenever he remembered the men laughing at him he felt a sharp, deep, burning flush of shame.

Far ahead on the road Sanu saw a great spot of orange. It moved and changed shape and it came closer. Then Sanu saw that it was a group of holy men from India.

With gleaming, shaven heads and bare feet they walked north toward the Himalayas, carrying only their begging bowls for luggage. Some of them wore white or red marks on their foreheads, which told what sect they belonged to.

When Sanu caught up to them he put the palms of his hands together and said, *"Namaste,"* and the holy men replied in the same way.

"You are going to the Himalayas?" Sanu asked.

"Yes, that is where we are going," said one of the holy men.

"And what do you hope to find there?" Sanu asked.

"Oh," said one of the holy men, smiling, "we know what we shall find. We are going to pray at the source of Mother Ganga—the holy river. And we shall find it."

Often people from India—simple peasants or holy men—went to the source of the great Ganges River which began in the foothills of the Himalayan mountains. Sanu knew that well. But still he liked to ask questions and to hear the answers. "And what else will you do?" Sanu asked.

All the holy men smiled now. "That is enough," said one of them. We have come all the way from southern India to do this one thing. That is quite enough for us."

Sanu said goodbye and went along the road remembering what the holy men had said. But he could still not think about anything clearly, because suddenly, surprising him with a sharp thrust of pain, came the memory of his humiliation.

Sanu walked along the road. Even though it was spring, the earth was dry and powdery. It was good for the pilgrims' feet, Sanu thought. Perhaps someday he would join the pilgrims or holy men. He could easily make the journey to the source of Mother Ganga.

When Sanu turned into the lane he was surprised to see three old neighbor-women sitting nearby in the shade. Sanu ran toward the house. In front of the door his grandmother was talking to Ram.

As soon as he saw her, Sanu knew that she was going away. In her hand she held a long

stick to help her walk, and tied to her side was a small cooking pot. Without being told, he knew that she was going to join the neighbor-women in the road.

"I was waiting to say goodbye to you," she said when Sanu came up to her, "but first I would like to know where you have been all morning."

"I—I have been to Katmandu," Sanu said as he looked at the dusty ground near his feet. He didn't know what to say and he was too ashamed to tell her why he had gone and what had happened. His grandmother waited. Then Sanu looked at her directly. "Let me tell you why I went to Katmandu some other time, please. Now tell me where *you* are going. Are you going to Ceylon? Are you going to make a pilgrimage to the Bo tree?"

"No, no . . . I am not going to Ceylon."

"But *why?*" Sanu asked in surprise.

"Ceylon is very far and I am very old," Sanu's grandmother said. "Now I am going to the source of the Ganga. That is something that is within my power to do."

Ram and Sanu walked with their grand-mother to the road. They watched her join the other women and begin the long journey to the north. "Hey, Sanu—" Ram called as his brother disappeared toward the fields.

But Sanu did not want to talk. He kept hearing his grandmother's words: "That is something that is within my power to do." Then he remembered the holy man saying, "That is quite enough for us." The words sounded over and over again in his mind.

Sanu took his hoe and began to work. The weeds were thick and growing fast. Sanu could destroy them so that the onion plants would become strong and fruitful. Yes, that was something he could do well—but certainly there was something else he could do.

He could not join the holy men or pilgrims on their long journeys. He could not go with the Tibetan traders. He could most definitely not climb with the potato-faced men to the Goddess of the Wind. And yet . . .

Sanu thought of the plump mastiff puppies in

the leather pouch he had seen a year ago. Some-way, somehow, he would try to get one. Perhaps two. And then, if he could breed them, he would have more puppies. Why couldn't he sell them just as well as the Tibetans? Was that something a boy could do? Sanu did not know. Only one thing he was sure of—that he must do something "within his power to do."

Sanu stopped to rest as the sweat poured down his cheeks. Somewhere to the north, beyond the dazzling white peaks of the closest mountains, was the Goddess of the Wind. Perhaps someday it would also be within his power to climb that high mountain. But that would come later.

ABOUT THE AUTHOR

Much of Arnold Dobrin's boyhood was spent in the sunny canyons and on the broad beaches of California. It was here —where the Asian influence is more pervasive than in other parts of the country—that his interest in Oriental philosophy first developed. His travels in the Orient (which led to the publication of books based on experiences in Thailand and Japan) increased his interest in the less well known countries of Asia.

For centuries Nepal had forbidden entry to foreigners, but in the mid-1950's a political upheaval returned the king to power and opened the country to the outside world. Mr. Dobrin was among the first visitors to Katmandu and the beautiful valley in which it is situated. *To Katmandu* is drawn from his experiences in that distant and still relatively unknown part of the world.